Welcome to ALADDIN QUIX!

If you are looking for fast, fun-to-read stories with colorful characters, lots of kid-friendly humor, easy-to-follow action, entertaining story lines, and lively illustrations, then **ALADDIN QUIX** is for you!

But wait, there's more!

If you're also looking for stories with tables of contents; word lists; about-the-book questions; 64, 80, or 96 pages; short chapters; short paragraphs; and large fonts, then **ALADDIN QUIX** is *definitely* for you!

ALADDIN QUIX: The next step between ready to reads and longer, more challenging chapter books, for readers five to eight years old.

Luna's Obedience School

Read the other book in the Pet Pals series!

Mitzy's Homecoming

PET PALS

Luna's
Obedience
School

by ALLISON GUTKNECHT

illustrated by ANJA GROTE

ALADDIN QUIX

New York London Toronto Sydney New Delhi

ALADDIN QUIX
Simon & Schuster Children's Publishing Division
1230 Avenue of the Americas, New York, New York 10020
First Aladdin QUIX paperback edition February 2022
Text copyright © 2022 by Allison Gutknecht
Illustrations copyright © 2022 by Anja Grote
Also available in an Aladdin QUIX hardcover edition.
All rights reserved, including the right of reproduction in whole or in part in any form.
ALADDIN and the related marks and colophon are trademarks of Simon & Schuster, Inc.
For information about special discounts for bulk purchases, please contact Simon & Schuster Special Sales at 1-866-506-1949 or business@simonandschuster.com.
The Simon & Schuster Speakers Bureau can bring authors to your live event. For more information or to book an event contact the Simon & Schuster Speakers Bureau at 1-866-248-3049 or visit our website at www.simonspeakers.com.
Cover designed by Laura Lyn DiSiena
Interior designed by Ginny Kemmerer
The illustrations for this book were rendered digitally.
The text of this book was set in Archer Medium.
Manufactured in the United States of America 1221 OFF
2 4 6 8 10 9 7 5 3 1
Library of Congress Control Number 2021941038
ISBN 9781534474024 (hc)
ISBN 9781534474017 (pbk)
ISBN 9781534474031 (ebook)

For Whiskers,

my first and forever friend

Cast of Characters

Luna (LOO-nuh): Cranky cat at Whiskers Down the Lane Animal Shelter

Gus (GUS): Large guard dog at the shelter

Buttons (BUH-tens): Shy kitten at the shelter

Mitzy (MIT-zee): Excitable toy poodle at the shelter

Ted (TED): Manager of Whiskers Down the Lane Animal Shelter

Frances Dinkle (FRAN-siss DIN-kuhl): Animal trainer

Contents

1

The Bite Buster

Luna growls the moment she sees the white coat.

She squints her round green eyes, pushes back her ears, and whips her tail from side to side. Then she lets out a long hiss.

"It's a vet! It's a vet!" **Gus** barks at the person who has entered Whiskers Down the Lane Animal Shelter. "Everyone, take cover!"

"I'm way ahead of you," **Buttons** whispers, already hidden under his blanket.

"Hello, Dr. Vet!" **Mitzy** says, welcoming the stranger. She balances on her rear legs, and paws at the bars of her cage. "Are you here to see me? Most vets come for me."

"You must be Ms. Dinkle." **Ted**

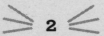

2

greets the woman. "I'm Ted, the manager here. We spoke on the phone."

"Ah yes." She shakes Ted's hand. "I'm **Frances Dinkle**, but you can call me the Bite Buster."

Ted laughs at her nickname. "That's exactly what we need. Let me introduce you to your **clients**."

"Clients?" Buttons asks. "I thought you said she was a vet."

"She *looks* like a vet," Gus insists. He lifts his snout and howls at the ceiling.

"We might as well start with Gus," Ted says. "As you've heard, Gus loves to bark."

"I am a guard dog!" Gus yaps.

"He's a great dog, and he would make a wonderful pet,"

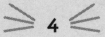

Ted explains. "But the constant barking is a real deal breaker for people."

"I understand why," the Bite Buster comments. She reaches into the pocket of her coat and removes a squirt bottle. **"Yeeeeeeep!"** Gus yelps.

The Bite Buster zaps a thin spray of water at his nose.

Ted's eyes widen. "We usually try to use a more positive approach with the pets in order to—"

The Bite Buster cuts Ted off. "Gus quieted down, didn't he?" She returns the bottle and moves over to Buttons's cage. Then she unlatches the lock and pulls the blanket off Buttons's **trembling** body. "Who is this fraidy-cat?" She lifts Buttons by the scruff of his neck and holds him in front of her.

"That's Buttons," Ted says. "He's only a few months old. The rest of his litter was adopted right away, but Buttons is shy. He hides around those he doesn't know well."

"One easy way to change that," the Bite Buster says as she lowers Buttons back inside. She closes him in and hands the blanket to Ted. "Get rid of this."

"Err, r-really?" Ted stammers. "But it seems to make Buttons feel safe and—"

"Next!" The Bite Buster crosses

the lobby toward Mitzy, who leaps up and down happily. "Look at this bundle of energy!"

"Mitzy! I am Mitzy!" She grips her squeaky purple ball and throws it against the grate. "Do you have any treats?"

"To be honest, Mitzy isn't a major challenge on her own," Ted begins. "She's very lovable and playful, even though she's one of our older pets."

"Then why is she still here?" the Bite Buster asks.

"Because of this one." Ted taps Luna's door, and Luna glares at him. "Mitzy and Luna were brought to the shelter together. They're very attached to each other."

The Bite Buster peers at Luna curiously. Luna's mouth remains closed at first, until a moan sounds from deep within her throat. She flattens her whiskers against her cheeks and crouches like she's ready to pounce. Then she shows the Bite Buster her fangs.

"Luna has some . . . anger issues," Ted explains. "She lashes out when she feels uncomfortable. Hissing, swiping, even biting— anything she can do to scare people."

The Bite Buster folds her arms over her chest. "You think you're tough, huh?" she addresses Luna.

"Try me," Luna yowls.

"Egh, she's nothing," the Bite Buster declares. "I can fix her."

2

Shape Up

Ted brings the Bite Buster into his office to sign paperwork, and she carries Buttons with her. After a few minutes Buttons flees, his tiny body **slithering** along the lobby floor like a snake.

"Thank goodness you escaped!" Gus howls. "I was afraid she catnapped you!"

"Why did *you* get to go with them?" Mitzy asks, annoyed that she wasn't chosen.

Buttons scurries into his cage, shivering. "The Bite Buster said I have to get used to being around people."

Gus cocks his head. "So she's not a vet?"

"She's an animal trainer," Buttons explains. "She owns an **obedience** school—that place where they teach us how to listen and do the right thing."

"Oh! I went to obedience school when I was a puppy," Mitzy says. "They taught me to stop peeing inside."

"You still pee inside," Luna points out.

"But not as much!" Mitzy argues.

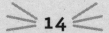

"Why is she here?" Gus asks. "We don't need obedience."

"Are you kidding?" Luna says. "Didn't you hear what Ted told her about your barking? She must be here because of you."

"Me?" Gus is shocked. "What about Buttons? She took his blanket away."

"That was very mean!" Mitzy agrees.

"Ted hired her to train all of us," Buttons says. "But she's going to work with Luna first."

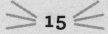

"Ha!" Luna cheers. "So she'll be out of our way in no time." She twitches her whiskers sharply. "I'll cough her up like a hair ball."

"No, Luna," Buttons corrects her. He peers around the room nervously. "I heard Ted say he's afraid that if you don't stop being mean, no one will ever adopt you."

"I don't care if I'm adopted," Luna insists, but her voice sounds shaky.

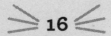

"But Mitzy wants to be adopted," Gus reminds her. "And she won't leave without you."

"That's what Ted said," Buttons continues. "Which is why if Luna doesn't change soon, she's going to be sent to a different shelter. So that Mitzy will have a better chance of finding a new home on her own."

Silence falls over the lobby as this news sinks in. After a few seconds Mitzy whimpers, "They cannot do that!" She looks at

Luna with concern. "Can they?"

Luna turns away and places one paw on top of her toy mouse, but she doesn't answer.

"Can they?" Mitzy repeats with more worry.

"They won't, if Luna behaves," Buttons says. "You can stop hissing, Luna. You won't scratch or bite people anymore. Right?"

Just then the Bite Buster exits Ted's office. "There you are!" She walks to Buttons, who tries to make himself **invisible**. "You can

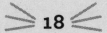

run, little fellow, but you can't hide. I'll see you tomorrow." She pats Buttons on the head roughly. Then she turns and points at Luna. "And you. It's time for you to shape up!" As Luna snarls, the Bite Buster slams the front door behind her.

"Luna!" Gus scolds. "You can't act that way anymore, or they're going to make you leave!"

"I can act however I please!" Luna argues, while Mitzy shuffles into a corner with her tail between her legs.

"Don't worry, Mitzy," Buttons assures her. "We'll help Luna figure out ways to be nicer. We'll make sure she passes the Bite Buster's test."

"NONSENSE!" Luna bellows. "I am already nice enough!" She

bangs her tail on the floor of her cage like a drumstick.

"You hiss at the volunteers!" Gus points out.

"Oh, that's all in good fun," Luna says, dismissing him.

"And you bit the last nurse who gave you a shot," Buttons adds.

"Well, I didn't want a shot," Luna counters. "It was a totally reasonable response."

"You swiped at my friend Dustin!" Mitzy cries.

Finally Luna doesn't have a comeback.

"Mitzy returned early from Dustin's foster home because of you," Gus says. "That boy smelled like bologna and powdered doughnuts. And she left him. For you."

Luna starts licking her chest, refusing to make eye contact. "I never asked her to do that."

Buttons perches at the edge of his open cage. "You didn't have to ask," he explains. "That's just what friends do."

3

Poodle Emergency

The next afternoon Ted escorts Luna, Mitzy, Buttons, and Gus into a large storage closet stacked high with cans of flaked tuna and bags of crunchy kibble and boxes of fresh-scented litter.

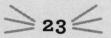

"Look at this place!" Gus barks with wonder. "It's magical!" He zigzags around, exploring the smells. "There is beef breakfast! And chicken breakfast! And turkey breakfast! And pork breakfast! And—"

"We don't need the full supply list," Luna says, interrupting him. She settles on top of a broken cage.

"Sit, Gus," Ted begs, but Gus is too busy sniffing a bacon-flavored package to listen. "Gus, come on. Gus!"

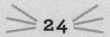

ZAP! A stream of water hits Gus's snout.

"Where did that come from?" Gus howls.

Buttons squeezes himself under a cabinet. "It's the Bite Buster!"

"Hello!" Mitzy calls as the Bite Buster enters, gripping a squirt bottle. Mitzy rests her front paws on the Bite Buster's knee. "I am Mitzy, remember? Did you bring treats?"

"You're sure you want to work with all four at once?" Ted asks the Bite Buster.

"I'm positive," the Bite Buster answers. "I think it's the best way for me to observe what **triggers** Luna to react."

Ted nods. "Sorry again about the tight space. We don't have a lot of extra room."

"I'll make do," the Bite Buster says. "You can leave us to it."

As Ted exits, Mitzy continues to trot over the Bite Buster's sneakers, trying to get her attention. "Hello! Ms. Buster! It is me, Mitzy! Down here!"

"Sit!" the Bite Buster instructs, and when Mitzy doesn't obey, she presses the dog's bottom to the floor. "Now stay!" She hands Mitzy a bone-shaped cookie from her coat pocket.

"Ooh! A treat!" Mitzy chews her reward and then follows the Bite Buster to the spot where Buttons is hiding. "Please can I have another one?" The Bite Buster kneels to peer under the shelves, and Mitzy licks the tip of her nose. "Pretty please?"

"No!" the Bite Buster yells, but Mitzy keeps running her tongue across the woman's face like it's a melting ice cream cone. "NO! NO! NO!"

Startled, Mitzy scrambles away. "I am sorry, Ms. Buster."

Luna arches her back and flexes her claws while her tail fluffs to double its normal size.

"Luna, do not pounce!" Gus

commands. "You have to be nice!" Slowly Luna pulls in her nails and straightens her spine, appearing to calm down.

"Good job," Mitzy says, praising her. "I am proud of you."

The Bite Buster tugs Buttons out of his hiding spot and cradles him like a baby. "You need to learn to be brave," she coos. "Here. I brought you a present."

"Excuse me." Mitzy paces in front of the closet door. "I have to go to the bathroom."

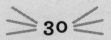

The Bite Buster places Buttons on the floor and dangles a ribbon above his head. "Go ahead," she encourages him. "Catch it!"

"Ms. Buster?" Mitzy pipes up again. "It is an emergency."

Buttons reaches one paw up to bat the end of the ribbon. "Good boy!" the Bite Buster compliments him.

Mitzy looks from the Bite Buster to the closed door and back again. "Well, I guess you are busy." She squats down and lets a puddle form between her rear legs.

Slowly the Bite Buster turns around.

"No! No! Bad dog!" The Bite Buster flaps her finger in Mitzy's

face. "We do not—**YOW!**" The Bite Buster spins and finds Luna clamped to her ankle, her sharp teeth grasping the skin.

"Back away from the poodle," Luna sneers.

4

Attack Pack

Once everyone has been returned to their kennels, Ted takes the Bite Buster into his office to talk. Luna sits cleaning her face, ridding herself of the Bite Buster's germs. Her friends stare at her, waiting.

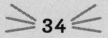

"Well?" Buttons interrupts the silence. "What do you have to say?" But Luna doesn't pause in grooming herself.

"Luna!" Gus yelps.

Luna's paw rests in midair as she scans the room. "Are you talking to me?"

"Of course we're talking to you!" Buttons shrieks. "You promised you wouldn't be nasty to the Bite Buster."

"I was perfectly polite," Luna argues.

"You bit her!" Gus points out.

"Oh please," Luna scoffs. "I didn't even break the skin."

"You still attacked her," Buttons says. "For no good reason."

"*She* had no good reason to scream at Mitzy," Luna replies, defending herself. "I was simply making things fair."

Mitzy lies with her chin between her front paws. "You cannot do that anymore. Or they are going to send you away." She turns her face to the side with a soft whimper.

Buttons begins circling his cage,

thinking. "We need a **strategy**. Something for Luna to do whenever she feels like biting."

"She can bark!" Gus suggests.

"Cats can't bark," Buttons reminds him. "But maybe she could purr?"

"I don't purr," Luna insists.

"Ever?" Buttons asks.

"No," Luna answers. "Purring is for the weak."

"How about if you meow?" Mitzy offers.

"Luna's meows sound like

threats," Buttons warns. "I think it has to be an action. Like instead of biting, you knead the ground."

"Or you spin in a loop," Gus offers.

"Or you jump in the air!" Mitzy pipes up.

"Those are **ridiculous** ideas," Luna protests. "When I feel like biting, I bite. End of story." With that, she carries her mouse to her bed, coils herself into a circle, and drapes her nose with the mouse's tail.

"That's it!" Buttons exclaims. "Your mouse!"

"Mouse?" Gus howls. "What mouse? Where is the mouse?"

"The toy," Buttons says to reassure him. "Luna, you're always kind to your mouse. So, what if whenever you feel like biting, you picture your mouse in your mind?"

BANG! Ted's office door slams into the wall as the Bite Buster barges out, two Band-Aids pasted above her foot. She stomps to

Luna's cage and grips the metal grid.

"Tomorrow's your last chance," she announces, before storming out of the lobby.

5

The Bodyguard

"You can do it," Mitzy coaches Luna the following morning.

"Remember," Gus adds, "if you make it through this lesson without biting, scratching, or hissing, the Bite Buster should let you stay."

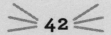

"Keep thinking about your mouse," Buttons encourages her. "You wouldn't hurt your mouse."

"All right, all right," Luna says. "Stop **badgering** me."

The Bite Buster opens Luna's door and scoops her up by the armpits. "It's only you and me today," she tells the cat. Luna's hind legs dangle beneath her, and she swishes her tail like a playground swing. But she doesn't make a peep.

The Bite Buster closes the two

of them in the storage closet and settles cross-legged on the floor. "Here. Take a whiff." She lets Luna smell her fingertips, and when Luna doesn't react, the Bite Buster scratches her between the ears. Luna's fur ripples at the touch, but she keeps her mouth shut.

"You're in a good mood today, huh?" the Bite Buster asks. "Let's see if you can keep it up." She strokes Luna's back, which makes Luna rise to her tiptoes. She then tickles Luna's chin, pats the base of her tail, and taps each of her paws with a **"Boop!"** But no matter what the Bite Buster does, Luna remains calm.

"Hmmm." The Bite Buster grabs a brush from the shelf. She runs it down Luna's spine and over her ears, up her tail and through her

whiskers. Luna squints her eyes closed. "You like to be brushed, don't you?" the Bite Buster asks. "You're being a good girl." She reaches into her pocket and hands Luna a crunchy treat. Luna gives it a long sniff, but she refuses to eat it. "Do you want a new flavor?" The Bite Buster offers two more pieces, but Luna stays as still as a statue.

"I'll leave you by yourself for a bit," the Bite Buster says, "in case you change your mind." The Bite Buster stands and exits, but even

after she's gone, Luna doesn't touch the treats. Instead she wanders to the far end of the closet, leaps onto the roof of the broken cage, and tucks her front paws underneath her.

After a few minutes the door reopens, and a fuzzy white cloud bounds inside. "Luna! It is me! Mitzy! Ms. Buster said you were very nice. She said we can play together now—ooh, treats!" Mitzy dives at the pile and chews one happily.

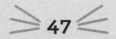

"NO! NO! NO!" the Bite Buster bellows. "Those aren't for you! Bad dog!" She bends toward Mitzy. **_HISSSSS._** In a blur of claws and fangs, Luna soars through the air.

6

Moving Day

"STOP!" Mitzy throws herself between Luna and the Bite Buster, knocking Luna off-balance right before her teeth make contact. Luna manages to land on her feet, and she grips the floor, her eyes

narrow with anger. "You promised you would try!" Mitzy scolds.

"I *did* try," Luna says, defending herself. "But I'm not going to
watch her bully you."

"Luna," Mitzy begins, "you do
not have to take care of me anymore."

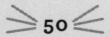

"This has nothing to do with you," Luna lies. "And everything to do with teaching that white-coated clump of litter right from wrong."

"Okay. I've seen enough," the Bite Buster says. "Out, both of you." She thrusts open the door and shoos them into the lobby. Side by side Luna and Mitzy walk to their cages. Luna enters hers, and Mitzy follows behind. They stand nose to nose inside the cramped space.

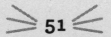

"What are you doing?" Luna asks. "Get into your own."

"If they send you away, they have to take me, too," Mitzy answers. Luna's jaw drops to protest, but she stops herself. Instead she lies on her bed and lets Mitzy curl around her, the dog's furry

head resting on Luna's neck. And despite herself, Luna starts to purr.

"The issue is worse than I thought," the Bite Buster tells Ted.

"Oh dear," Buttons cries.

"We can stop this!" Gus barks. "We won't let her take Luna!" He hurls himself against the walls of his kennel as the Bite Buster reaches for the squirt bottle. At the sight of it, he quiets down instantly.

"But I have a **solution**," the Bite Buster continues. "Luna needs to

be moved to a different location."

"Noooooooooo!" Mitzy moans, tightening her grip around Luna's ribs.

The Bite Buster approaches Buttons's cage and rests her hand on its lock. "I suggest placing Mitzy next to Buttons, and Luna next to Gus," she explains. "From what I've seen, Luna mostly acts out when Mitzy is involved, as if it's her duty to protect the dog. Separating them— even if just across the room—might do everyone some good."

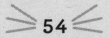

"Noooo—" Mitzy begins to cry again before coming to a fast halt. "Wait a second. So you are not making Luna leave?" She scampers over and paws at the Bite Buster's knee. "Luna can stay here?"

The Bite Buster pets Mitzy's head gently. "How would you like to live next to Buttons?"

"I would like that very much!" Mitzy says before returning to Luna. "But I am going to miss you."

"I'll be ten feet away," Luna points out. "You can look at me all day if you want." She pauses. "But please don't."

"I will teach Gus how to clean your ears for you," Mitzy promises her.

"I am a guard dog, not a cat groomer!" Gus pipes up. "But I do have one question, Luna: What are your plans for that mouse?" He shudders ever so slightly.

Luna swats at the toy, and it slides between Mitzy's legs. "You keep it. So that Gus doesn't throw a fit."

"I will take excellent care of it," Mitzy assures her.

"Give it to Buttons," Luna offers. "Maybe it will help him be brave."

Mitzy lifts the mouse by one of

its ears. "That is very **generous** of you."

Luna looks away, suddenly feeling shy. Then after a moment she whispers, "That's just what friends do."

Word List

badgering (BA•juh•ring): Annoying without stopping

clients (KLIE•uhnts): Those who hire professionals to help them

generous (JEH•nuh•russ): Giving freely

invisible (in•VIH•zuh•bull): Not able to be seen by others

obedience (oh•BEE•dee•uhnts): The state of being willing to obey

ridiculous (ruh•DIH•kyuh•luss): Very silly

slithering (SLIH•thuh•ring):
Sliding like a snake

solution (suh•LOO•shun): A way
to solve a problem

strategy (STRA•tuh•jee): A careful
plan

trembling (TREM•bling): Shaking
and shivering

triggers (TRIH•gers): Causes a
response

Questions

1. Why does Luna need obedience training?
2. What does the Bite Buster do to Gus when he is barking?
3. How did Buttons discover the reason why Ted hired the Bite Buster?
4. What does Buttons suggest Luna picture in her mind whenever she feels like biting?
5. What do you do to calm yourself when you are feeling angry?

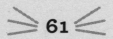

6. How do you think Luna and Gus will get along? What about Mitzy and Buttons?

7. Which pet from Whiskers Down the Lane Animal Shelter would you most like to live next door to? Why?

QUIX FAST★FUN★READS

LOOKING FOR A FAST, FUN READ?
BE SURE TO MAKE IT ALADDIN QUIX!

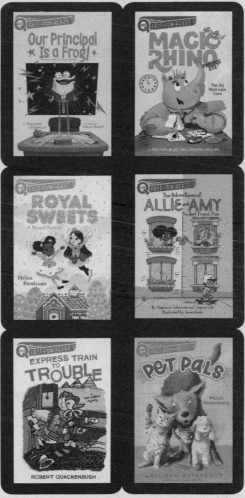

CHUCKLE YOUR WAY THROUGH THESE EASY-TO-READ ILLUSTRATED CHAPTER BOOKS!

EXTRAORDINARY WARREN
A SUPER CHICKEN
PIX
by SARAH DILLARD

EXTRAORDINARY WARREN
SAVES THE DAY
PIX
by SARAH DILLARD

SNAIL HAS LUNCH
PIX
by MARY PETERSON

BUCK'S TOOTH
PIX
Diane Kredensor

THIS LITTLE PIGGY
AN OWNER'S MANUAL
PIX
Cyndi Marko